THE HEIGHTS

CAMP

THE HEIGHTS

Blizzard
Camp
Crash
Creature
Dam
Dive
Heist
Jump
Mudslide
Neptune
Ransom
River
Sail
Shelter
Score
Swamp
Treasure
Tsunami
Twister
Wild

Original text by Ed Hansen
Adapted by Mary Kate Doman

ISBN-13: 978-1-61651-284-2
ISBN-10: 1-61651-284-9
eBook: 978-1-60291-698-2

Printed in the U.S.A.

21 20 19 18 17   10 11 12 13 14

Chapter 1

Antonio and Franco were in the garage. They were packing supplies. The Silva men were going camping! They would hike. And fish. And camp. It would be great. The boys always wanted to go to Montana.

"Montana has good fishing. There's a lot of fish," Antonio said.

"I know. We'll catch a lot. Then we'll grill them," said Franco. "It will be our dinner every night. I hope you like trout!"

"I love trout! I'm glad Dad is taking us," Antonio said.

"Me too. I can't wait to camp," agreed Franco.

Antonio had a list. He didn't want to forget anything.

"Two fishing rods," Franco said.

Antonio checked it off his list.

"Bug spray," said Franco.

"Check," Antonio replied.

Rafael loaded the car with their bags. Ana and Lilia helped too. There were a lot of bags. But soon they were off!

Ana and Lilia waved goodbye. They didn't like fishing. They would stay home in the Heights.

"Bring us back some fish!" Ana said.

"Will do!" Antonio yelled.

"Love you Mom! Lilia!" yelled Franco.

They got to the airport fast. Franco saw their plane.

"I'm glad I have something to read. It's a long flight," Franco said.

"Brought my DS," Antonio grinned.

"I've got a couple of movies," Rafael replied.

Antonio asked his dad about bears. "I hope we see some," he said.

"There are bears in Montana. There are grizzlies. And there are black bears. We may see some," Rafael said.

"Great!" said Antonio. "What about deer?"

"Yes, deer, too," Rafael said.

"Mule deer, right Dad?" Franco asked.

"Yes, they are very big," said Rafael. "I hope you brought your cameras!"

The boys looked at each other.

"Oops! We forgot," said Franco.

"That's okay," Rafael said. "We can buy one."

Finally, they arrived. The airport was crowded.

The boys got the bags. Rafael got the rental car. They were on their way.

Rafael stopped at a store. "We'll get more supplies here," he said.

"Antonio, look for a camera. Franco, grab some snacks. Meet me at the checkout."

Antonio got a camera. Franco got snacks. Rafael paid the bill. They all packed the car.

Chapter 2

It was a beautiful day. The air was cool. The sun was bright.

Franco and Antonio were excited. They loved camping. They couldn't wait to see wild animals. Fishing would be fun too!

"There hasn't been rain for weeks. We have to be careful with our campfire. Look how dry everything is!" Rafael said.

They entered the canyon. Rafael slowed down. Big Sky Motel and Restaurant was on the left. The Silvas got out. They looked around. Mountains were behind the motel. A man walked up to them. He wore a cowboy hat and boots.

"Welcome to Big Sky! I'm Nate," he said.

Rafael said hello. He shook Nate's hand.

"These are my sons Antonio and Franco," said Rafael.

"Is this your first trip to Montana?" Nate asked.

"Yes. I can't wait to see some animals," said Antonio.

"Is that so? Well, you've come to the right place. Let's get your things to your room," Nate said.

The room was small. But it was clean. And it was comfy. The Silvas unpacked. Rafael pulled out a photo of Ana and Lilia. Now the room felt like home.

Then they went to the restaurant. They were hungry. It had been a long day. The food on the plane was bad. Nate's wife Helen was there. She took their order.

"We're hungry! Buffalo burgers for us all!" Rafael said.

"And fries," Franco added.

"And ice cream!" yelled Antonio.

"Coming right up!" Helen laughed.

The buffalo burgers were great. The fries were salty and fresh. The ice cream was homemade. They ate everything.

Nate came over to their table.

"What animals do you want to see?" asked Nate.

"Grizzly bears," Antonio replied.

"Talk to Ray Johnson," Nate said. "He knows all about grizzlies. One even bit part of his leg off!"

Antonio's mouth dropped open. His eyes were wide.

"No way!" Antonio said. "Where can we find him?"

"You're in luck," Nate laughed. "He's right behind you!"

Chapter 3

Ray Johnson was tall and thin. He walked with a limp, but he looked strong and scary.

Antonio walked over to him.

"Are you Ray Johnson?" Antonio asked.

"Yeah. What's it to ya?" Ray asked.

"We're here camping. We want to see a grizzly. Nate said to talk to you," said Antonio.

"I do know a lot about grizzlies," Ray agreed.

Rafael and Franco walked over.

"Would you tell us about them? I'll buy your dinner," Rafael said.

Ray looked happy. He liked talking about bears. He liked free dinners too!

"Sit down. What do you want to know?" Ray asked.

Ray told them about grizzlies. He talked about their size and strength.

"They are very fast," said Ray. "People can't outrun them."

Ray knew a lot about bears. Antonio wanted to know everything. He wanted to know about their claws. He wanted to know about their teeth. He was very interested.

"Grizzlies aren't scared of anything. They will walk up to you," said Ray. "Most are over 1,000 pounds!"

"What do they eat?" asked Antonio.

"Thirteen-year-old boys, "grinned Ray.

Was this true?

Antonio looked at Ray. He looked at Ray's leg. Ray winked.

"What happened to your leg?" Antonio asked.

Ray stopped talking. He looked at Antonio.

"You're the first person to ask. Everyone looks away. No one talks about it. You have guts, kid," grunted Ray.

“Thanks, I guess,” laughed Antonio.

Ray told the Silvas about the grizzly attack. “It happened eight years ago. I was alone in the forest. I hadn’t seen a bear all day. Then I turned a corner. I walked into a mother bear and two cubs. The mother charged. She knocked me over. I rolled into a ball.”

Antonio pictured it in his head.

“The bear clawed my leg. Her paw sliced it open. Then she left,” said Ray.

The Silvas were tired. It had been a long day. They heard enough of Ray’s stories. Antonio really did not want to see a bear. Not anymore!

“Thank you, Ray,” Rafael said.

"You told us a lot! But how do we avoid bears?"

"Make lots of noise," said Ray. "Use pepper spray."

They all said goodbye.

Antonio was quiet. He looked scared.

"I hope I never see a bear!" he said.

Franco and Rafael laughed.

Chapter 4

“Aaahh!” Antonio screamed. He sat up in bed. He was shaking.

“What’s going on?” Franco asked.

“Franco! I had the scariest dream,” cried Antonio. “A huge bear attacked me!”

Franco yawned. “Go back to bed. There aren’t any bears in here.”

But Antonio was still scared. He couldn’t fall asleep. He tossed. He turned. Then it was morning.

The Silvas ate breakfast. Antonio told his dad about the dream.

"Don't worry," said Rafael. "A bear won't get you. Ray scared you."

"I guess you're right," Antonio said.

The Silvas got ready to leave. They packed up. Their campsite was far. Helen waved to them.

"Have fun. Be safe. Be careful with your campfires. The forest is dry," said Helen.

"We'll stop at the bait shop," Rafael said. "We'll get more supplies. Then we're off!"

The bait shop was busy. A lot of people needed supplies.

"Hi," said a girl. "My name is Tory. What can I get you?"

“Good morning. We need some bait,” said Rafael.

“Have you ever seen a bear?” Antonio asked.

“Many times. I saw three last week,” Tory said.

Antonio looked scared.

“Don’t worry,” said Tory. “They weren’t grizzlies. They were black bears. Grizzlies are brown.”

Antonio didn’t know that. Grizzlies had brown fur. They had big claws. They had sharp teeth.

“Climb a tree if you see a grizzly. It can’t get you,” Tory said.

“Good tip,” Rafael said.

“Do you have pepper spray?” asked Franco.

“Yes. It keeps bears away too. Clip

it on your belt. You can grab it fast,"
Tory said.

The Silvas got pepper spray. Rafael clipped it on his belt. Antonio felt better. He wasn't scared of grizzlies anymore. Dad could spray it if he saw one. The spray stung. The bear would run away.

"Thanks Tory," Rafael said.

"No problem," Tory replied. "Here. Take this too."

Tory handed Rafael a book. It had pictures of footprints. They were animal footprints. Antonio looked at grizzly footprints. They were big. They looked scary.

Chapter 5

The ride was hot. It was dusty. They drove to the trail. They would hike to the lake. They would set up a campsite. And they would sleep there.

Franco unpacked the car. Antonio filled the backpacks. Rafael got the water. They had a lot of supplies. Their backpacks were full. They had a tent. They each had a sleeping bag. And they had food for six days. The backpacks were heavy!

A sign ahead read:

WATCH OUT
FOR GRIZZLY BEARS

Antonio thought of Ray. He thought of the bear attack. He thought of his dream. For a second he was scared. Then he thought of Tory. She didn't see a grizzly last week. Antonio wasn't going to be scared. They had pepper spray. His brother and father were there. He was ready. Just in case...

The Silvas hit the trail. It was dusty. The trees were tall. Everything was a little brown. They climbed uphill. They passed streams, plants, and trees. Antonio and Franco were happy. They wanted to get to the lake. It was nice out.

Swimming in the lake would be fun. The day was warm. There wasn't a cloud in the sky.

Rafael and Antonio were tired. But not Franco. He ran a lot for football. He was in good shape. Soon they stopped for a rest. They stopped by a stream. Rafael looked at the map.

"We don't have far to go," Rafael said. "The rest of the way will be easy. The trail is less steep."

Franco passed out food. Everyone was hungry. They ate fast.

Antonio walked by the stream. He saw footprints in the mud. He looked at them. They looked like a man's foot. A man who was very big. Antonio looked closer. He saw something. It looked strange. The footprint wasn't right. The toe wasn't where it should be. It was outside the foot.

"Hey Dad! Franco! Come here," he yelled. "Look what I found!"

Rafael and Franco ran over. Antonio pointed to the footprints. They all looked. Rafael got the footprint book.

"A bear made that track," Franco said. "Look at this. Bears have their big toe on the outside."

"Look for claw marks," Rafael said. "Black bears have claws close to their toes. Grizzlies claws are far from their toes."

Antonio studied the tracks.

"Black bear," he said.

"Good," said Rafael. "You're

learning to read prints. Okay, ready to go?” Rafael asked. “We still have a three-hour hike.”

“Let’s go!” Franco said. “I can’t wait to get to the lake.”

Chapter 6

The Silvas got to the lake at 5:00 p.m. Franco and Antonio ran to the water. Antonio jumped in. He splashed Franco. The water felt good. It was cool. The boys were tired from hiking.

"Hey guys, come on! We need to set up camp," Rafael yelled.

Franco and Antonio didn't want to get out. But they knew they had to. It was getting dark. Their dad needed help. Antonio splashed Franco one more time.

"We need to set up the kitchen first. It needs to be by the water," said Rafael.

The Silvas set up the kitchen fast. They didn't have too much food. They would eat the fish they caught.

Next, they needed a sleeping area.

"We can't sleep near the kitchen. In case a bear comes," said Rafael. "We don't want it to think we're food!"

"Let's put the tent by that tree. We can climb it if a bear comes," Antonio said.

"Great idea, Antonio!" said Rafael.

"You're learning a lot."

Franco started to laugh.

"What's so funny?" Antonio asked.

"It's a lot of work to hide from bears. I feel like we're in a movie," said Franco. "I guess I can't have a midnight snack!"

"You can sleep by the food. I may sleep in a tree!" Antonio said.

"We keep the food up in another tree. That way a bear can't get it," said Rafael.

"Oh man!" said Antonio. "I give up. Maybe we shouldn't keep food anywhere!"

Now Franco looked scared. "No food for a week? I'll take my chances with a bear!" Franco laughed.

Rafael hid food in a tree. Antonio

found a flat spot for the tent. It was perfect. A tree was close by. It had low branches. And it was easy to climb. They raised the tent. They unrolled their sleeping bags.

Chapter 7

The Silvas woke up. It was early. And the sun was bright. They had all slept well. They all ate breakfast. Now they were ready to fish.

"I bet I catch the first fish!" Franco said.

"You're on," said Antonio.

The boys ran to the lake. Antonio got there first. He threw his line in. Franco was right behind him.

Antonio felt his line pull. It was a fish! He caught one already.

"Hold tight. Pull it up!" Rafael said.

Antonio reeled the fish in. The fish fought hard. But Antonio held on tight. The fish got tired. Antonio pulled harder. The fish stopped fighting. Antonio grabbed a net. He scooped up the fish. It was a trout.

"Good job, Antonio!" Rafael said.

"I caught the first fish. I won the bet," said Antonio.

"You sure did. That was fast. I didn't have a chance!" agreed Franco.

They caught more trout. Antonio and Franco each caught five. Rafael caught three. The sun rose high. The fish stopped biting.

"Let's go on a hike," Rafael said.

They put their fishing gear away. They cleaned their catch. And they walked into the woods.

Franco looked at a rock. He saw something move. It had brown and white ears. It's tail was long and pointed.

"Look! It's a weasel!" Antonio said.

The weasel ran up a tree. The Silvas left.

"Okay, where should we hike?" Franco asked.

"Let's follow this stream," Antonio said. "We can look for tracks."

They walked up a hill. It opened to a field. Rafael stopped.

"Don't move." Rafael said.

"There's a bear."

Antonio didn't move. He thought of his dream.

"Maybe he won't see us," Franco said.

"Look! There's a tree," Antonio said. "We can climb it."

"Walk to the tree," Rafael said. "Walk fast! And be quiet."

"Stay down and move fast!" whispered Franco.

Antonio was scared. But he made it to the tree. He started to climb.

They looked at the bear. It had a hump on its back. Its ears were small. It had silver fur around its neck. Oh, no! It was a grizzly!

Chapter 8

Antonio watched his dad. Rafael walked to the tree. He was fast. He was quiet. Antonio knew he'd make it.

"The bear won't see him," Antonio thought.

Then Rafael stepped on a twig. It made a loud noise. The bear turned around. It saw him. It ran toward Rafael! Antonio saw the bear's teeth.

He heard it growl. It was just like his dream.

Rafael ran toward the tree. He ran fast. The bear was faster. Rafael grabbed the pepper spray. Then he tripped over a rock. Rafael dropped the pepper spray. He fell. The bear got closer.

Antonio had to help! He jumped out of the tree. The bear saw him. It growled. Antonio ran to his dad. The bear looked mad. Antonio saw the pepper spray. He picked it up. The bear was above him. Antonio aimed the can at the bear. He pushed down.

Pepper hit the bear's face. Antonio sprayed its eyes. The bear was blinded. But not for long. It ran toward the water. Pepper got into Antonio's eyes. It stung! But everyone was okay.

"Franco, take care of your brother," Rafael ordered. "I'll make sure the bear is gone."

Franco jumped out of the tree. He ran over to Antonio.

"Antonio, you were great! Dude, you scared him away!" Franco yelled.

"Which way is the water?" Antonio asked. "This stuff stings!"

Franco led Antonio to the stream. Antonio washed his eyes. The cool water felt good. His eyes still hurt. They were red too. At least he could see!

"Wow! Tory was right. That stuff works!" said Franco.

"No sign of the bear. Good thing

we met her," Rafael said. "Or we'd be bear food!"

"Let's get back to camp," said Antonio. "I like it better there."

The Silvas headed back to the lake. They walked fast.

Antonio thought about the bear. He thought about Ray. The Silvas were lucky they got away.

They were happy when they reached camp. They were hungry. And tired.

"At least we'll eat a good dinner," said Franco.

"Again with the food," teased Antonio.

"I need to eat. It's for football," grinned Franco.

They all laughed.

Franco was right. Dinner was great. The Silvas cooked their trout.

"This is the best trout I ever ate," Franco said.

Rafael and Antonio agreed.

After dinner they cleaned up. They put the food up high in the tree. Nobody wanted the bear to come back!

It got dark fast. The Silvas looked up at the stars. There were thousands of them. It was a nice night. They all fell asleep fast. It had been a long day!

Chapter 9

Miles away, there was smoke. And there was fire! But the Silvas were deep in the woods. They didn't know this. They left the lake before the smoke. Rafael wanted to hike to a fishing stream. It was 10 miles away. Not many people went that far.

"It's a hard hike. But we can do it," Rafael said.

"That sounds cool," Antonio said.

"But I'm holding the pepper spray."

They packed fast. They started hiking before 8 o'clock. Rafael was right. It was a hard hike. They hiked for five hours. They set up camp. Soon it was time to fish!

The stream was small. So they fished far apart.

"Let's not get too far apart," Franco said. "I want to be near the pepper spray."

The fishing was great. They caught a lot of fish.

The wind was blowing hard. Soon the fire was moving. It was burning through the forest.

"Look!" Antonio yelled. "Two deer are crossing the stream."

Franco saw something too. It was

a fox.

Rafael heard a noise. He saw a moose crossing the stream too. “What’s going on?” he wondered.

“Listen! What’s that noise?” Antonio asked.

They all stood still. Rafael and Franco heard the noise too. They didn’t know what it was.

“I smell smoke,” Franco said.

Two more animals ran past them. Rafael knew what was happening. It was a forest fire!

“We have to get out of here!” Rafael shouted. “It’s a fire! It’s headed this way. That’s why the animals are running.”

The Silvas ran to camp. They packed their camping gear fast.

By now the smoke was strong. And the sky was dark.

"Look, Dad!" Antonio yelled. "The fire's almost here!"

Rafael stared at the flames. All he could see was fire. Smoke filled the air. It was hard to breathe.

Rafael looked at his sons. "Forget about the gear!" he yelled. "Leave everything! Run!"

The air was hot. Sparks flew all around. Everywhere a spark landed, there was fire. Franco saw burning trees.

"Hurry up! The fire is moving fast. We're going to have to move even faster," Rafael yelled.

"Dad," Franco groaned. "The fire is catching us."

“Keep moving,” said Rafael. “We have to find an opening in the flames.”

A huge tree crashed in front of them.

“Try to jump over it!” Rafael yelled.

Franco jumped over easily. So did Rafael. But Antonio fell. He was on the ground. The flames came closer. Sparks fell on his shirt. He started to smoke.

Chapter 10

"Oh no!" Antonio yelled. "I'm on fire!"

Franco had seen Antonio fall. He jumped back over the burning log. He pulled his brother up.

"This way, Franco!" Rafael screamed.

Franco threw Antonio over the log. Rafael reached out. He grabbed him. Rafael patted down Antonio's smoking clothes.

"Are you okay?" asked Rafael.

"Yeah! I just tripped," Antonio croaked.

Franco jumped back over the log.

It was hard for the Silvas to breathe. They covered their noses and mouths.

"At least we're faster than the fire," Rafael thought.

It was very dark. Rafael hoped they were going the right way. He wanted to be near the lake.

"We're close. We can make it," said Rafael.

"The smoke is bad," Franco said. "It's hard to breathe."

They were getting tired. They slowed down. Antonio struggled to keep up. The flames were getting closer.

“We’ve got to go faster,” Rafael thought.

Franco ran ahead. He stopped to look around.

“Dad, I see the lake!” yelled Franco.

“We made it!” Rafael shouted.

They all ran fast. They jumped in the lake. The water was cool. It felt great. Rafael looked back at the fire. It had reached the lake. Now it moved around the water. They all stared.

“Wow!” Rafael said. “That was close.”

“Yeah,” Franco said. “This trip has been crazy!”

“We can’t get out yet,” Rafael said. “We have to wait. I know it’s cold. But it will be light soon. And the fire will be out.”

“Trips with you are never boring,

Dad," said Franco. "We've had some exciting times."

"Yeah! And some times have been too exciting!" Antonio laughed.

"I want you to know I'm proud of you guys. We ran into a lot of trouble. You both helped out," Rafael said.

At first light they swam to shore. The fire was out.

The Silvas hiked down the mountain. They found their car. It was okay.

"You know what Dad?" Antonio said. "Now I know why Mom likes the Heights. Nothing crazy ever happens there! She won't believe this."

"Oh, yes she will," said Rafael. "She is used to our crazy adventures by now."